PHIL OF THE FUTURE™

Stuck in Time

Adapted by Jasmine Jones

Based on the television series, "Phil of the Future", created by Douglas Tuber & Tim Maile

Part One is based on a teleplay written by Tim O'Donnell

Part Two is based on a teleplay written by Adam Lapidus & Steve Luchsinger

Watch it on
Disney CHANNEL
abc kids.

DISNEY PRESS

VOLO

New York

Printed in the United States of America

First Edition
1 3 5 7 9 10 8 6 4 2

Library of Congress Catalog Card Number: 2005921379

ISBN 0-7868-4725-5
For more Disney Press fun, visit www.disneybooks.com
Visit DisneyChannel.com

PART ONE

CHAPTER ONE

"I'm just going to use these holograms to pick out some school clothes for the kids to wear tomorrow," Mr. Diffy told his wife as he fiddled with the oval-shaped gadget in his hand. Mrs. Diffy nodded in complete agreement.

Living in a new century meant wearing new clothes. Every time traveler knew that. And the Diffys were a time-traveling family. Unfortunately, at the moment, they also happened to be a time-traveling family stuck in time.

Blending in was the first order of business. At first, the Diffys didn't think it would be all that hard. After all, they didn't have gills, or four arms, or pointy ears, or anything like that. They were just your average, ordinary family from the year 2121, whose Fleet Flyer just happened to malfunction on its way back to the Age of Dinosaurs.

Once Mr. Diffy realized they were stranded, he'd bought his family a typical two-story house in the suburbs and disguised their time-travel machine as an RV parked in front of it. Now all he had to do was figure out the clothing thing for his kids.

Mr. Diffy shook the Wardrobe-o-gram and pressed a button. It beeped and projected two shimmering holograms in front of him—one of his son, Phil, and the other of his daughter, Pim. The two glowing figures were dressed like Pilgrims in drab black outfits. Pim gathered her long skirts and curtsied in a gesture of coy politeness, which was extremely *un*-Pim. And Phil looked unnaturally stiff in his old-fashioned getup.

"That doesn't seem right," Mr. Diffy said with a frown. "Let's try this." He pressed another button, and Phil and Pim were suddenly wearing scuba gear. The Phil hologram began to move his arms as if he were doing the breaststroke.

Mrs. Diffy frowned and scratched her head as she gazed at the scuba outfits. She wasn't one hundred percent sure about it—but she had seen a few movies set in the twenty-first century, and most of the ones about school *hadn't* taken place underwater.

"Lloyd, I don't think those are school clothes, either, sweetheart," Mrs. Diffy said to her husband as Phil and Pim wandered into the living room and flopped down on the couch.

"School!" Pim shrieked. "Did I hear you say '*school*'? Are you kidding? We actually have to mingle with these twenty-first-century knuckle-draggers?"

Pim had never wanted to come to the twenty-first century in the first place—or the Age of

Dinosaurs for that matter. Her first time-travel choice had been ancient Egypt, where she was convinced her blond hair would make people think she was a goddess—now, *that* was Pim's idea of a vacation!

Unfortunately, the time-travel laws under the International Unification Treaty of 2095 strictly forbade anyone from visiting a time period in which they would stand out—so Mr. Diffy had nixed that. And then, of course, the time machine's wave generator went bust.

"Look, kids, I don't know how to tell you this," Mr. Diffy said slowly. "I'm not sure how long it's going to take me to fix the time machine, so your mother and I have decided to enroll you in school."

Phil and Pim exchanged uneasy looks.

Mrs. Diffy nodded with enthusiasm, as if twenty-first-century school was going to be some sort of thrill ride. "Phil, you're going to be in something called the 'ninth grade,'" she explained, trying to make school sound like an adventure. "And Pim, you're going to be in something called the 'seventh grade.'"

Pim's eyes narrowed. "*I* want to be in ninth grade."

"Honey," Mrs. Diffy said patiently, "they go by *age* here."

"All right," Pim said slowly, with a smug I'll-play-your-little-game smile. "I'll start in your seventh grade. Then I'll begin my slow but steady rise to power." Pim leaped to her feet and shook her fist in the air. "In a month, I'll be in fiftieth grade!"

Phil stared at his little sister and sighed. How in the world is Pim supposed to fit into this time period? he asked himself. The girl's already weird in our own century!

With a grunt, Phil yanked Pim back down on the couch. "Dad," he said, "we need more information about how school works in this century before we just jump in."

Mr. Diffy smiled confidently and held up the Wardrobe-o-gram. "I'm doing the research," he promised. "By tomorrow morning you two will know everything necessary to be just a couple of normal American kids."

The next day, Phil and Pim strutted through the front doors of H. G. Wells Junior/Senior High. Phil sported a wide-brimmed blue hat with a long feather in the band, gold chains, dark glasses, and a blue cape. Pim wore a feathery hairdo, round sparkly shades, and a green-and-brown outfit made up of about three tons of polyester.

The night before, their dad had assured them that this was the way to blend in with the "groovy" kids of this time zone. And Phil and Pim had believed him. They'd spent hours learning gestures and vocabulary.

Now, as the two Diffys swaggered through the hall, Phil felt completely confident. He flipped back the wings of his blue cape, exposing his bright orange polyester shirt. "Solid, bro!" he called to a passing boy.

The boy didn't respond. He just gaped at Phil. Slowing their walk, Phil and Pim finally took a serious look around. A knot of guys in jeans and T-shirts stood gawking at them. A group of girls wearing miniskirts stood in a corner, whispering and pointing.

Okay, thought Phil, here's an observation: number of dudes in capes—zero.

Pim had come to the same conclusion. She smirked at her brother. "Dad hosed us," she said.

Phil sighed. "You think?"

CHAPTER TWO

As Phil and Pim filled out registration forms in the principal's office—and mutually agreed to dump the old-fashioned slang their dad had taught them—the morning classes at H. G. Wells began.

In the ninth-grade math class, a popular girl named Tia stood in front of the blackboard staring blankly at the numbers, letters, and fractions. "Are you *sure* this is a ninth-grade problem?" she asked the teacher. "I mean, this is, like, *professional* algebra."

Miss Hanks rolled her eyes. "It was last night's homework," she snapped. "Did you actually *do* any of it?"

Tia's eyes widened in mock horror. "Of course," she insisted.

Miss Hanks frowned, clearly doubting it.

"Keely and I were going to," Tia finally admitted, "but . . ." She desperately searched out her best friend for help.

"We needed to concentrate," Keely quickly spoke up from her desk, "so we went to get a smoothie. But then we couldn't remember which Vitamin-Boost makes you smarter, so we got all of them. But then we drank them too fast and our faces froze up." Keely crossed her pretty hazel eyes, imitating a frozen face.

The class burst into laughter. Tia laughed the hardest.

"You think it's funny?" Miss Hanks asked, glaring at Tia. "Well, you're not leaving that board until you figure out the problem."

Keely winced. She'd thought her funny story

would help her friend—but it looked like she'd only made Miss Hanks angrier. Of course, the real truth wasn't so funny. She and Tia had been totally stumped by the very first home-work problem. So they'd bagged the whole thing and given each other makeovers instead.

Oh, well, thought Keely, as she admired the hot-pink streak in her friend's hair, maybe we can't do algebra, but at least we're *lookin'* good!

Just then, Phil Diffy opened the classroom door and strolled in. He had ditched the blue hat and cape, but he was still stuck wearing his orange polyester shirt, red pants, and white belt. The outfit was better suited for a 1970s disco dancer than a present-day ninth grader.

"And who are you?" Miss Hanks demanded.

"Phil Diffy. I'm new here." He gave the teacher a big, friendly smile.

"New?" Miss Hanks frowned and searched the pile of papers on her desk. "How come I never get those memos?"

As Miss Hanks searched through her

attendance papers, Phil noticed Tia standing in front of the blackboard with a confused expression on her face. He scanned the complicated math problem on the board. "X equals nine," he told her.

"X equals nine?" Tia repeated with a scowl. That is the weirdest pickup line I've ever heard, she thought.

"Actually," Miss Hanks said with a smile of surprise, "that's exactly what it is, Tia. X equals nine." She nodded at the equation on the chalkboard. "And *you* had *all night* to figure it out. And Mr. Phil Diffy here, our new student, he got it *right away!*"

Phil shrugged. "Well, actually . . ." he began, and then stopped himself. He was going to tell the teacher that he'd learned algebra in Level Beta, ages ago, and the equation on the board was pretty basic for him. But then he'd have to explain that he was, like, over one hundred years ahead of these kids—and that would probably blow the whole "blending in" thing.

As Tia skulked back to her seat beside Keely, Miss Hanks beamed at Phil. "It's a pleasure to have you in class," she told him.

"It's great to be here," Phil said. "I love math."

Keely rolled her eyes at that one. "Who loves math?" she whispered to Tia.

Tia smirked. "And who'd *admit* it?" she pointed out—obviously nobody with whom she'd want to associate.

Miss Hanks pointed to another equation on the board. "Would you like to try our extra-credit problem?" she asked Phil.

He looked over the other problem. It was much longer and more complicated.

"It's for math lovers only," Miss Hanks added.

"Well, I guess I could give it a try," Phil said. He approached the board, picked up the chalk, and weighed it in his hand uncertainly. Back home, he used a laser pen and handheld videogram to solve equations.

This chalk thing is way weird, he thought. Talk about *old*-school! Still, the math itself hadn't changed, he decided. Well, not *much*. Unless you were talking about the kind of equations required for travel in the fourth dimension.

With quick movements, Phil tackled the problem. His hands picked up speed as he started to see his way through the equation— and as he got used to working with the chalk, of course. A few moments later, Phil stood before the board, the problem elegantly solved before him.

A guy in the back of the room with a mop of wavy red hair stood up and began to applaud.

Geez, Phil thought worriedly. Maybe I should have pretended like it was a little harder.

"That was fantastic!" Miss Hanks tossed Phil an off-the-charts huge grin. "Why don't you take a seat behind Miss Teslow?" She pointed to Keely.

Phil nodded at the cute blond girl and slid into his seat.

Tia leaned toward Keely and whispered, "Good. Math dweeb is sitting behind you."

Keely turned to sneak a glance at Phil. Well, she thought, his outfit is wack, but you have to hand it to the guy—when it comes to math, he has serious game.

Phil noticed Keely looking at him, and he gave her a big grin. She quickly turned away.

"There's one guy I won't have to worry about for the test tomorrow," declared Miss Hanks, pointing to Phil. "As for the rest of you?" She winced. "Keely and Tia—oy!"

CHAPTER THREE

While Phil was acing ninth grade, Pim was suffering through seventh. As she walked into her next class, a prim girl in a pastel sweater set and crisply ironed skirt approached her and declared, "Hi, you must be new! I'm Debbie Berwick."

Debbie stuck out her hand. Pim eyed it coldly. "What am I supposed to do with that?" she asked.

Debbie giggled. "Well, shake it, silly!"

Pim grabbed Debbie's thumb and gave it a

waggle. Debbie stared, too polite to point out that Pim's hand-shaking wasn't exactly up to the standards of Miss Manners. "If you need any help getting to your other classes, I can show you around," she said instead. "I'll even take you to the only cold drinking fountain. It's a long walk but, gosh, it's tasty!"

Pim narrowed her eyes suspiciously at Debbie. She never trusted people who were perky and friendly—they usually had ulterior motives. "Look, I don't know what your angle is," snapped Pim, "but keep it in your backpack."

"Okay, now!" the teacher, Mr. Hackett, announced. "We've been in school for less than a month and already I'm missing nine pounds of chalk." He stared at the class with a serious expression. "That's a whole lot of chalk, people. And it's not walking away on its own. So, apparently, from now on, I need a chalk monitor. Volunteers?"

Debbie's hand shot up.

Oh no you don't, Pim thought, shooting her

own hand up a second later. Obviously, this chalk-monitor thing was a huge deal. And Pim wasn't about to let Little Miss Debbie Sunshine walk off with the honor.

"Kudos, Berwick," Mr. Hackett said. "You had your hand up first."

What? Pim thought in outrage. She glared at Debbie, who stood up and smiled. "Thank you, Mr. Hackett," she said earnestly. "Wow, this is so unexpected!" She turned to address the class. "Now, I want you to know that during my reign . . ."

Mr. Hackett rolled his eyes. "Sit down, Berwick. You're chalk monitor, not Miss Tennessee."

Pim leaped out of her chair. "That's it?" she demanded. "That's how you're going to decide who gets to be chalk monitor? Is that how George Washington got elected? He stuck his hand up and went 'ooh, ooh, pick me, pick me.'" Pim glared at the teacher as a murmur of agreement rippled through the class.

Mr. Hackett dubiously gazed at his new student. "Oh, I see what this is," he said finally. "This is one of those *stalls* to get out of work. But I'm in a good mood today, so what the heck. Tomorrow we'll have an election for chalk monitor and everybody can feel important."

Debbie smiled sweetly at Pim, who smirked back, thinking, Take that, you knuckle-dragger! No sickeningly chipper girl from ancient history is going to stand in my path to power. Any day now I'll advance to grade fifty!

Later that day, Phil experienced twenty-first-century cafeteria food, which was . . . *interesting*, even if it was difficult to identify. But it was hot and most likely nutritious, so he loaded up his tray.

Tia, Keely, and their girlfriends seldom lowered themselves to go through the lunch line more than once a week. They preferred takeout.

At the moment, Tia was batting her eyelashes

at the Thai-food delivery guy. By now she knew him by his first name.

"Marty," she said, "you're a *dream* for going back for the peanut sauce."

Marty smiled as he handed her the small plastic container filled with the Thai condiment.

"Yeah," Keely added, "we're thinking of going Italian tomorrow. When we decide, we'll shoot you a fax."

Marty nodded and departed. Then Keely followed Tia back to their usual table on the lunch patio, which was covered in opened take-out containers. Keely and Tia's posse of the ultra-cool were already picking at their food with chopsticks.

"You think we'll ever get in trouble for ordering off-campus?" Keely asked.

Tia pouted as she slid into her seat. "What are they going to do? Arrest us for having better taste than everyone else?"

"Hey there," said a voice. Keely looked up into a pair of smiling brown eyes.

"I'm Phil."

Keely and Tia looked at each other.

"From your algebra class," Phil added. As the two girls stared blankly at him, his smile faltered. Hmmm, he thought, maybe I'm not making it clear enough that I want to be friends. Maybe, in this century, you have to spell things out. He decided to try again. "Well, first off, I just wanted to say I love your school, and look forward to getting to know each of you as individuals." Nobody leaped at the offer, so Phil decided to sweeten the deal. "And second, if anyone needs help with algebra, I've got nothing but free time."

"Tell you what," Tia told him. "Leave us your card, and we'll let you know."

"Yeah," Keely agreed, looking away. "We're fine. Thanks."

"Okay," said Phil. He sighed. Well, that didn't go so well, he thought. I wonder if I said something that offended them. Or maybe I should have greeted them with a catchy phrase from this historical time period—I can see I have some studying to do.

Turning to another table, Phil noticed the guy with the floppy red hair from his algebra class, the one who'd clapped when he'd solved the extra-credit equation. After class, the kid had introduced himself as Seth Wosmer. Well, thought Phil, at least there's one kid in school who seems interested in friendship with me. Er, at least, I hope so. . . . "You, uh, mind if I grab a seat?" Phil asked hesitantly.

Seth scooted over, clearing room on his bench. "I'd be honored if you grabbed mine."

Okay, so that worked, Phil thought as he sat down beside Seth. Maybe the problem isn't with me. Phil frowned over at the table where Keely and Tia were sitting. "What's going on with the people over at that table?" he asked.

Seth rolled his eyes. "That's the *popular* table," he explained. "You were in way over your head."

Phil lifted his eyebrows in surprise. "I was?" he asked.

Seth gave Phil a confused look and said, "Don't tell me you didn't have cliques at your old school?"

"My old school?" murmured Phil. He considered telling Seth the truth about his education. Basically, he'd lie back in a Comfa-cliner every day and check out the preprogrammed lessons on the Virtu-teacher.

For a moment, Phil's mind went back to the history lesson he'd been watching the day before he and his family had taken off in the Fleet Flyer 6000. . . .

Across his visor screen, elephants trumpeted as men in armored breastplates and helmets drove them forward through rough terrain. In the corner of the screen, the Virtu-teacher popped up to narrate.

"So, Hannibal assembled his army of elephants and prepared to cross the Alps," the Virtu-teacher explained.

Suddenly, her face broke into a huge grin. "We'll be right back with the conquest of Europe right after this!" The image behind the teacher swirled and changed, and in the next moment, the Virtu-teacher was standing in a green pasture, surrounded by black-and-white cows.

"Doesn't history make you thirsty?" the Virtu-teacher asked. "It does me. That's why I reach for a nice, refreshing Cheeseola— sparkling soda combined with the great taste of cheese!"

Ah, Cheeseola, Phil thought. Gosh, I wish I had one of those right now. . . . He looked at Seth and cleared his throat. "You might say my old school was way different," he explained.

Seth nodded. "Okay, then pay close attention to how it works here at Herbert G. Wells Junior/Senior High: those"—he pointed to Keely and Tia's table—"are the popular kids. They're at the top of the food chain. Beneath the popular kids . . ." Seth turned and gestured to a cluster of guys with thick necks wearing varsity jackets and girls with pom-poms. ". . . there's the football team . . . followed by the ski squad . . ." He pointed to guys with long hair and ski caps. ". . . the student government kids . . . the soccer studs . . . the air-guitar posse . . ." Seth heaved a sigh. "And then guys like us who dig algebra."

Phil shook his head in disbelief. "Seth, that's awful."

"Don't worry," Seth said. He smiled knowingly. "According to Mother, one day, you and I are going to *own* these people."

Phil looked around the lunch patio and frowned. I don't want to own them, he thought. I'd just like to talk with them.

CHAPTER FOUR

"Cupcake, Glen?" Debbie asked. She pulled a gooey treat out of her basket and handed it to a classmate passing by her in the hall.

"Berwick!" Pim snarled, striding up to her chalk-monitor opponent.

"Would you like a cupcake, Pim?" Debbie asked innocently, holding out the basket.

"And if I take one, I'd have to vote for you for chalk monitor?" Pim asked sarcastically.

Debbie's eyes grew wide. "No," she insisted. "I'm not trying to bribe people. These are leftovers. Twice a week I get up early and I take homemade cupcakes down to the nursing home. See?"

Pim looked down at the cupcake Debbie had just thrust into her hand. There was a message scrawled across the top in frosting. "'Hip replacements rock,'" Pim read aloud as Debbie wandered off with the basket of sweet treats. "All right, Berwick," she growled under her breath, "you want to throw around bribes? You're on."

"I'm on?" Debbie asked, turning around. "I'm on what?"

How did she hear that? Pim wondered. Okay, cover. "You're on . . ." Pim struggled to come up with something. ". . . a wonderful path of enlightenment."

Debbie smiled. "Mmmm, thank you!" She pranced off to hand out more treats.

Pim watched her go, eyes narrowed. "And that path leads you right over a cliff," she quietly snarled.

"Oh, dear, that sounds dangerous," Debbie said, turning around again.

What the—? Pim wondered. How did she *hear* that?

"Umm, maybe we should choose a different path," Debbie suggested.

"Different," Pim repeated. "Right. One that leads to a field of flowers and a big rainbow!" she said brightly.

"Yeah!" Debbie agreed. She turned a corner with her cupcakes.

"And in that field," Pim said in a super quiet whisper, "you'll be pushing up daisies."

"I sure hope so," Debbie called in reply, popping her head back around the corner. "I love daisies!"

"What does she have, like, *bat* hearing?" Pim cried.

"Follow me," said a voice behind Phil. A moment later, Keely was walking in front of him, looking straight ahead.

"What?" Phil asked.

"Don't turn around," Keely commanded without moving her head.

"Am I being kidnapped?" Phil joked.

Keely didn't laugh. "Just walk, look straight ahead."

Phil couldn't think of any reason not to follow Keely. In fact, he was curious to find out what she was being so secretive about. Besides, for a historical person, she was very pretty. So he marched down the hall in lockstep behind her.

Turning a corner, Keely looked around. Once she saw that they were alone, she turned to face Phil. "This is good," she said. "I'd like to take you up on your offer to tutor me in algebra."

Phil's eyes widened in surprise. "You would?" he asked.

Keely nodded. "My mom will completely freak if I pull a D in there. I mean, I know I can do it, but I have trouble focusing. I can focus in English. You know, Charles Dickens. 'It was the best of times, it was the worst of times . . .'" She smiled. "I mean, c'mon—make a decision: which was it?"

Phil nodded, although he wasn't altogether sure what Keely was babbling about. "So, algebra?" he prompted.

Keely blinked. "Right. Can you help?" she asked.

"Sure. Great." Phil grinned. "Meet you in the library?"

"No, no. The library's too noisy," Keely said quickly. "How about . . . Otto's Pink Pig?" she suggested.

"Excuse me?" asked Phil. Maybe he'd missed something about the customs of this century, but he couldn't see how studying algebra had anything to do with farm animals.

"It's a restaurant," Keely explained as the bell rang for class. "Corner of Second and Brustrom. Meet me there at six." Then she hurried away.

The moment she had turned the corner, Phil

punched his fist in the air, then grooved into a few of those 1970s dance moves he'd studied the night before. Suddenly, he noticed that a crowd had gathered around to watch the kid in the polyester outfit get down to the music nobody else could hear. Phil cleared his throat. "I gotta boogie," he said, then hurried off to his next class.

"Pim," Mrs. Diffy said as she leaned against the kitchen island later that evening, "if you need brownies to win this election, I'm only too happy to help."

Pim surveyed the kitchen, which looked like it had been ransacked by a giant chocolate blob. Broken eggs and gooey chocolate batter were everywhere—including all over Pim's face and in her hair. So far, her mother's "help" hadn't done much good. Making brownies from scratch is complicated! Pim thought miserably. She'd even had trouble getting the stupid box open.

But after an unbelievable struggle, Pim and Mrs. Diffy had finally gotten the brownies into what they thought was the oven.

Unfortunately, they'd confused the oven with the dishwasher. The knobs had looked the same, and both appliances had similarly hinged doors. So, of course, the mix-up was understandable.

Mrs. Diffy took a deep sniff. "Wow, those brownies smell so good," she said. "Can't I just check on them?"

"For the last time, Mom, no," Pim said in exasperation. "The box says leave them in the oven for thirty-five minutes."

Mrs. Diffy picked up the timer and turned the knob to zero. *Ding!* "Ready!" she chirped with a grin. She and Pim hurried over to the dishwasher and yanked open the door.

Pim frowned at the tray of brownies. "Doesn't look like the picture on the box." The brownies were pretty runny . . . and, uh, *soapy.* Pim couldn't really figure out how this oven thing was supposed to work. How were soap-suds and running water going to cook anything? This twenty-first-century technology didn't make any sense. "Maybe this oven's broken," she told her mother.

Mrs. Diffy pressed her lips together. There was really only one solution here, she thought: revert to the twenty-second-century method of cooking. "Sweetie, I know that you want to win over your classmates," she said, pulling a can from the cupboard, "but why don't I just *spray* you some brownies?"

Mrs. Diffy removed the can's top and pressed the nozzle. A stream of thick, brown mist oozed out onto the counter. In mere seconds, the cloud turned solid, forming a plateful of delicious-looking, ultrachocolate, frosted brownies.

"With a nice cherry on top!" Mrs. Diffy sang, just like the Virtu-teachers did during commercial breaks in Pim's daily lessons back home.

"Bing," Pim added, watching the bright red cherry appear on top of the brownies.

Mrs. Diffy held out the Insta-food can to tempt her. "You want to lick the nozzle?" she asked.

"Mom!" Pim complained. "These have to be homemade. People in this century love homemade junk. Apparently it's 'to die for,'" she added, rolling her eyes and putting finger quotes around the words.

Actually, it was Debbie who'd told Pim that homemade treats were "to die for." Well, whatever, Pim thought. Debbie should know. They sure seem to be working for her.

Mrs. Diffy released a disappointed sigh. "All right," she said. "Let's give it another try."

"Hey, have you seen Phil?" Mr. Diffy asked as he walked in the back door carrying a chunk of the time machine's engine. "I need him to help me recalibrate the time machine's wave generator."

"He's at a place called Otto's Pink Pig," Mrs. Diffy said, "hanging out with a new kid he met at school."

"Great!" Mr. Diffy snapped in exasperation. "Is he wearing a sign that says, 'I'm from the future. Capture me, put me in the zoo'?"

Mrs. Diffy laughed. "Honey, relax," she said.

"I am not going to relax until we're back in our own century safe and sound!" Mr. Diffy insisted. "Anything that distracts us, even for a minute—" He caught sight of the spray can on the kitchen island. "Ooooh, brownies." Pressing the nozzle against his lips, he squirted himself a mouthful. "Mmmm," Mr. Diffy said through a giant chocolate bite. "I'll be out in the garage."

Pim shook her head as she watched him walk through the back door. "And that's the guy in charge of getting us home?"

CHAPTER FIVE

At Otto's Pink Pig, men in lederhosen and women in German folk dresses danced and clapped to the sounds of an accordion. Phil observed the spectacle with curiosity from one of the restaurant's big horseshoe-shaped booths.

Wow, he thought, no wonder twenty-first-century school is so backward. The places where the students study are really distracting. On the other hand, he was here with Keely, so he wasn't about to complain out loud.

With a smile, Phil turned his attention back to the lesson—and the plate of raw vegetables he'd been using as a study aid. "So," he said to Keely, "if two X are these two little radishes, how do you solve for Y?"

Keely stared at the vegetables on the table in front of them and thought for a moment. "Umm."

"Come on," Phil gently coaxed. "You know this. Remember," he prompted, "the olive is one point five."

"Multiply it by the olive?" Keely guessed. She looked up at him hopefully.

"Yes." Phil grinned. "So, 'two radishes' times 'one olive' equals . . ."

"Three celery sticks!" Keely blurted out, excitedly brandishing the vegetables.

"Yes!" cried Phil.

Keely considered the celery in her hand. "Three celery sticks," she said, almost to herself. "I never had anyone explain it like that. It's so easy."

Grabbing a piece of celery, Phil snapped it in half and offered Keely a piece. "Want a fraction?" he teased.

Keely giggled. No wonder this guy loves math, she thought as she ate the celery stick. He knows how to make it fun!

Just then, a large, bald man in a pink embroidered shirt walked up to them. "*Guten Abend*," the waiter said with a heavy German accent. "Welcome to Otto's Pink Pig. Before you sample my schnitzel, you must join me on dancing floor, yah?"

"No, thank you," Keely said with a smile, "but *Guten Abend* right back at you anyway!"

"Aw, c'mon, he's talking schnitzel!" Phil cried. If I have to dance for my dinner, so be it, he thought. The food at Otto's Pink Pig smells way better than the stuff my mom's always spraying up for dinner. Besides, I'm game for a new experience, especially with Keely.

He grabbed Keely's hand and pulled her onto the crowded dance floor. Then he joined the front line of folk dancers, hopping up and down and imitating their movements.

"Very good!" the waiter said with a booming laugh. "Very good!"

For a split second, Keely was horrified, but then Phil swept her up in a lively polka, and she started to laugh.

What am I worrying about? Keely thought as she danced around the floor with Phil. It's not like Tia or anyone else from school is going to see me here. For once, I can just do whatever I want!

It was a good feeling, she realized.

Once the song was over, Keely and Phil went back to their booth. "Wow, that was amazing," Keely said to Phil as she scooted around the horseshoe of the vinyl seat. "Where did you learn German folk dancing?"

Phil laughed as he slid in beside her. "I learned it just now, with you," he told her.

Keely smiled. She'd never met anyone like Phil before, she realized. He didn't seem to be afraid of anything. It was kind of amazing, really.

Suddenly, the restaurant's front door opened and Tia walked in, followed by a few other members of the school's popular posse.

Keely couldn't believe her eyes—or her bad luck. "Oh no!" she said with a gasp.

"What?" Phil followed her gaze. But he couldn't see any problem. "Hey, look, it's your friends from school!" He happily waved, trying to get their attention.

"Phil!" Keely cried in alarm. "Can I see you under the table for a minute?"

"Under the table?" Phil asked. "Why under the ta—Ooh!" Keely wasn't playing. She'd yanked Phil by the collar and pulled him down.

Under the table, Phil studied Keely's frowning expression and decided this *wasn't* a quaint custom from her century. "I'm sensing something's the matter," he told her.

Keely winced. "Yeah, kinda," she admitted. "I mean, you know how it is with cliques."

Phil shook his head, accidentally bumping it on the underside of the table. "Actually, I don't," he said. In the twenty-second century, Virtu-teachers had eliminated the need for traditional school—and therefore school cliques. But he didn't tell Keely that. Instead he asked, "Why are they such a big deal?"

Keely thought for a moment, but she couldn't come up with a good answer. "They just are," she said finally. "And there are rules. Lots of them. And here's the most important one—you can only hang out with people in your own clique. Period."

"Well, why?" asked Phil, honestly confused. "That seems stupid."

Keely frowned. She had to admit that it did sound kind of stupid. But it was the unwritten law of school. It was just the way things worked—and if you didn't play along, there were always consequences. Everyone knows that, she thought. At least, everyone I know. So why doesn't Phil?

"You know, you ask a lot of questions for a new kid," she said. "*Where* did you say you were from?"

"Uh, Montana," Phil quickly lied. "Actually, Canada. Spent some time in Mexico. Things were a little different there."

"Well, *here*, cliques are huge," she informed him, firmly.

"Oh." Phil looked into Keely's face. Her hazel eyes looked really pretty beneath the table—with the white tablecloth hanging behind her as a backdrop.

She's so pretty, Phil thought. And there's something about her. She's sweet . . . and smart, too . . . I really like her, he realized with a pang. And she likes me. We get along great. It should be really simple. But I guess that things in this century are more complicated than that.

"So I guess it would be bad for you to be seen with me," he said finally.

Keely looked away. "Kinda," she murmured.

Phil nodded. "All right. See you around, then," he said, starting to get up.

"No!" Keely grabbed his arm. "Tia will see you. Wait here. I'll check to see if the coast is clear." She rose up and peeked out.

"Keely?" squealed Tia, catching sight of the top of her friend's head poking up from under the table. Okay, she thought, that's weird. But she walked over to join her friend, anyway. "We're at this morgue 'cause we have an interview with this German dude about his culture for social studies," Tia explained, rolling her eyes to show how ridiculous it was. "But, girl, what are *you* doing here?"

"Uh," Keely said, stalling as she pulled herself up onto the booth's vinyl seat, "just studying for algebra. All alone." She laughed nervously. "Just me."

"So, can we slide in?" Tia asked.

"Actually, I just finished eating and was taking off," Keely lied, just as the waiter walked up to her with an enormous platter of food. That had been Phil's order. He'd been really excited about the schnitzel, for some reason, Keely remembered.

"One über-platter," the waiter announced as he plopped the food down in front of her, "*und* a side of curly fries."

"Oh," Keely said as she stared at the heaping platter. "I, uh . . ." She peered up at a very confused-looking Tia. "You know, I forgot I ordered . . . dessert."

Keely's heart nearly stopped as Tia and their friends Hayley, Courtney, and Brianna suddenly began to slide into the booth. She winced, waiting for them to declare in horror that there was a total math geek hiding under the table.

But they didn't say a word.

Confused, Keely peered under the table. Phil was gone. When she looked back up, she finally saw him—walking out the door.

CHAPTER SIX

"I care about our nation's chalk!" Debbie chirped the next day as students trickled into Mr. Hackett's class. "Hi, vote for me, I care about our nation's chalk. . . ."

"Look out!" Pim hollered as she hauled an enormous pan of fudge brownies through the classroom door. It had taken her four tries and six hours, but she had done it! She'd made enough of the delicious-looking chocolate treats for her entire class—without one single spray from a twenty-second-century Insta-food can. And, even more impressive, she'd managed to keep her mother from sneaking a single nibble. Now she was ready to pass the sweet little bribes out and reap the rich rewards of being elected chalk monitor.

"Brownies comin' through!" Pim cried as she plopped the huge pan onto Mr. Hackett's desk with a thunk.

Pim's wide-eyed classmates gathered around.

"Wow, Pim," Debbie said as she peered at the brownies, "looks delish. I usually don't sample my opponents' treats, but may I?"

Pim batted her eyes. I can afford to be gracious, she thought. Now that I've got this election in the bag. "You may," Pim declared.

Debbie reached over to break off a piece. No go. She really threw her weight into it, but the brownies wouldn't budge.

"I . . . I'm sure it's not rock hard," she told Pim apologetically. "My bony little fingers are probably just too weak."

Mr. Hackett pulled a long wooden ruler out

of his desk. "I got it. Yeah." He tapped the top of the brownies with the ruler. "Usually these babies have a sweet spot . . ." *Knock, knock, knock* went the tip of the ruler. "Aha!" cried the teacher when he came to a knock that sounded a little more hollow than the others. He stabbed the brownies with the ruler, which broke in two.

Mr. Hackett frowned for a moment. "Okay!" he exclaimed, and reached for the metal globe beside his desk. He raised the globe high then gave the brownies a solid whack! The globe bounced off the brownies and landed on the floor with a clatter.

Pim stared at her pan of beautiful brownies. They looked better than good. They looked perfect. But they were harder than titanium! These evil treats have betrayed me, she realized in horror. How could this happen? In 2121, I'm a genius, she thought. But in the twenty-first century, I'm totally humiliated because I can't work the primitive appliances of an old-fashioned kitchen!

Mr. Hackett rolled his eyes. "Okay," he said finally. "Everyone who wants Debbie for chalk monitor, raise your hand."

"Wait!" Pim cried. I can still win this election, she told herself. I just have to sink to the lowest level possible and play on their stupid notions of sympathy. I've seen plenty of examples on their daytime television dramas.

Pim heaved a sigh, imitating one of this era's actresses. "What was I thinking?" she said, pretending to hold back tears. "You're right. I cannot bake as well as Debbie Berwick."

Mr. Hackett sat back in his chair. "You got that right, sister," he agreed.

"I'm a pathetic fool for believing I could win the election," Pim went on in her tragic voice. "That I could finally have something *meaningful* in my life." She sniffled and wiped at a nonexistent tear. "Why should I miss being chalk monitor? I don't miss getting presents at Christmas. . . ."

Pim snuck a look around. Sure enough, her

classmates were misting up. *Yes*—they totally feel sorry for me! she thought.

"Or even one lousy card at Valentine's Day," she continued sadly. "And on my birthday, I don't even mind singing to myself: 'For she's a jolly good fellow,'" Pim murmured miserably. "'For she's a jolly good fellow . . .'" One of her classmates blew into a tissue. Even Debbie Berwick appeared touched. "'For she's a jolly good fellooooooow . . .'" Pim looked around. There wasn't a dry eye in the house. In the bag, she thought triumphantly.

"Okay," Pim said quickly, "let's vote!"

"I had the naughtiest dream last night about an improper fraction," Seth admitted to Phil as they walked toward their lunch table.

Phil shot Seth a confused look. "And?" he prompted. But just then Keely stepped in front of him. "Oh, hey," he said in genuine surprise. He hadn't expected her to talk to him ever again.

"Phil, guess what?" Keely said with a smile. "I got a B on the algebra test. I know it's not an A, but it's not a D. My mom's *so* going to want to put it up on the fridge." She giggled. "I'll probably let her. Anyway, I just wanted to say, 'thanks.'"

Phil smiled and nodded. "Then I just want to say, 'you're welcome.'" He started toward his table.

"Also, I'm sorry about last night," Keely quickly added as she fell into step beside him. "I was really rude."

"Hey. Don't worry about it," Phil told her, even though he thought it *had* been really rude. He liked Keely a lot, and he'd felt bad about what happened. But this wasn't his century, he reminded himself. He was just a visitor in it. "I'm sure it's not easy being popular," he added.

Tia rushed over. "Come on, Keely," she said without even bothering to glance at Phil and Seth. "Let's go to the table. Brianna's masseuse is coming to do our feet."

Keely started to follow her friend, but suddenly she stopped and turned back to Phil. "Well, I'll see you around," she said.

Phil nodded.

"Keely, come *on*," Tia urged. But for some reason, Keely couldn't make herself move.

Maybe it was the polka dancing, or the way Phil had explained algebra using celery sticks. Maybe it was the way his big brown eyes had looked at her so innocently underneath the Otto's Pink Pig table . . . but whatever it was, there was something about this guy Keely just couldn't walk away from.

She plunked her tray down onto his table and said, "Hey, do you mind if I sit with you and, uh . . ." She glanced at the redheaded kid from her algebra class.

"Seth Wosmer," he said in awe.

Tia stared at this scene in horror. "Keely, why are you sitting there?" she demanded.

"Because I'm having lunch with Phil and ah—" Oh, man, Keely thought. That redheaded kid's name just flew out of my brain again. I guess I'll have to get used to paying attention to him.

"Seth Wosmer," Seth volunteered.

Keely nodded.

"Keely, are you serious?" asked Tia. "I mean, because people are going to talk. You know, I can't have people talking."

Keely rolled her eyes. "Tia, who cares?" she snapped. "Who made up all these rules anyway about who sits where?"

Groaning, Tia glanced over at the popular table. She was going to miss the foot massage. But Keely was her best friend, after all. "Promise me this is a *one*-time deal," she said as she plopped down beside Keely.

"Wow!" Phil cried, grinning at Keely. "This is a major breakthrough. I mean, there's no reason why people can't eat outside their social groups. Life is short." He pounded his fist on the table. "What are we waiting for?"

As Seth, Keely, and Tia stared, Phil stood up.

Then he climbed on top of the table and pointed to one of the thick-necked jocks wearing varsity jackets.

"Hey you, Mr. Football," Phil called, "go sit with that band guy. And you!" He pointed to a tall guy in a blazer. "Aren't you from the Glee Club? Go scoot over there and sit with the kids from Metal Shop. And you with the pom-poms—" He pointed to a girl with thick glasses. "Have you met the girl hiding behind her laptop?"

Nobody moved.

"Uh, Phil . . ." Keely whispered up at her new friend. "It's not happening."

Phil looked around. Keely was right. In fact, everyone was gawking at him as though he'd just been beamed down from a distant world. Which was actually pretty close to the truth.

Phil climbed off the table and sat back down. "All right, well, you can't change the world all at once," he declared.

Keely nodded. "How about one table at a time?"

From his seat, Seth stared at Tia as though he were sitting in front of the most beautiful quadratic equation in the universe. "Seth Wosmer," he said, holding out his hand.

Tia crinkled her nose with mild disgust as she shook hands with Seth. "Hi," she said. "Nice to meet you, Seth . . . Wosmer."

"This is going right up on my Web site!" Seth cried.

Phil grinned. I actually kind of feel like I've made history, he thought. Small and insignificant history . . . but history nonetheless.

Just then, Phil felt someone tapping him on the arm. He found Pim standing next to him. "Phil, I just got a note from the office," she said. "It's from Dad. He says it's time to go home."

Phil's eyebrows drew together. "Home?" he repeated. "In the middle of a school day?"

"*All the way* home," Pim said meaningfully. Grabbing his arm, she dragged Phil away from the table. "We gotta go!"

* * *

Twenty minutes later, the Diffys were strapped inside the Fleet Flyer time machine parked in front of their house.

"Everyone buckled in?" Mr. Diffy asked as he scanned the readouts on the panel in front of him. "Anomaly sequencer . . ." Phil's father ran through the takeoff checklist as he flipped buttons and turned knobs. "Check . . . nitrogen boosters, check . . ." He held up his hands, inspecting them with a smile. "Cool driving gloves, check."

Phil sighed. His dad had discovered the twenty-first-century relic known as the "shopping mall," and gotten seriously into their selection of sunglasses and accessories.

"Okay, as soon as we're time-borne, I'll uncloak," Mr. Diffy went on, "and our time machine won't look like a goofy RV anymore."

Mrs. Diffy sighed. "You know, I gotta say, I'm going to miss this century," she confessed.

"Tell me about it," Pim agreed. She smiled

smugly, remembering how she'd won the chalk monitor election by a landslide. "I had those weepy pea-brains eating out of the palm of my hand."

An image of Keely flashed through Phil's brain. "I never got to say good-bye . . . " he murmured, half to himself. "And I'd just made history, too. . . ."

"Fire up the view screen . . . " Mr. Diffy said as he stared at the monitor that appeared where the usual windshield would be. "There we go." Phil's dad flipped one final switch, and the time machine started to rattle and shake. Phil felt himself fall slightly backward as their Fleet Flyer began to lift off.

"Yee-haa!" Mr. Diffy cried triumphantly. "I did it! We're zooming through time at warp speed!" He stared at his readouts and frowned. "But if we're flying through time at warp speed, why are all my readouts flat?"

Phil's dad undid his seat belt and poked his head out the time machine's door. "Whoa!" A burly guy had just hooked up their recreational vehicle to a tow truck, and was about to haul it away.

Mr. Diffy looked at the parking sign posted by the curb. "Ah! No parking on Tuesdays!" he cried. "I didn't see the sign." He turned back to his family and sighed. "Sorry, guys. Looks like we're going to be here awhile."

Phil wasn't all that disappointed. In fact, when he realized he'd be seeing Keely again, he couldn't help but smile.

For Pim, however, smiling wasn't something she'd be doing anytime soon. In fact, *coughing* was mostly what she found herself doing by the next afternoon. Now that she'd been elected chalk monitor, she was responsible for clapping every last eraser clean in the courtyard after school.

Will this torture never end? she asked herself amid yet another chalk dust coughing fit. Is *this* the twenty-first century's payoff for being gloriously elected to a high office?

"Wow, Pim," said Debbie, walking up to her. "You are doing such a great job as chalk monitor."

Pim stopped clapping erasers to glare at her rival. "Thanks," she snapped.

"Well, I'll see you tomorrow," Debbie merrily chirped, giving Pim a little wave.

Pim watched her go. "This is not over, Berwick," she whispered through gritted teeth.

"Of course it isn't, silly," Debbie called back cheerfully. "You still have a whole other box to clap!"

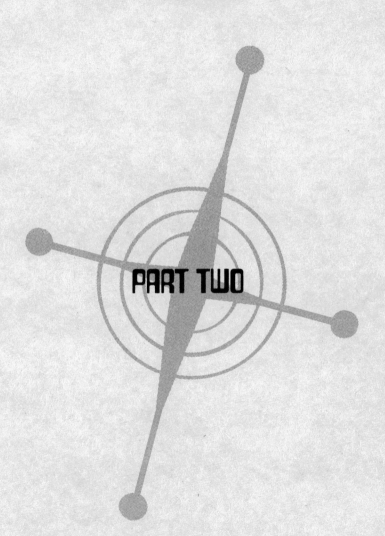

PART TWO

CHAPTER ONE

Pim pulled an animal cracker from the bag and inspected it. This elephant has no trunk, she thought. "Broken!" She tossed it onto the front lawn beside her feet, where it lay in a pile of rejected snacks. Leaning back against the wooden lounge chair, she pulled out another animal.

"Broken." Pim tossed it aside and tried another . . . and another and another. "Broken, broken, broken, broken, broken!" The pile of rejects grew larger.

In the twenty-second century, Insta-food spray cans made things like broken crackers a thing of the past. But now that Pim was *living* in the past, she had to put up with all kinds of annoyances—like these substandard animal crackers. So far, not one of them looked like the photos on the front of the bag.

Who wants to eat a lion without a head, or a giraffe without a leg? she thought in disgust. Finally, she pulled out a perfect specimen—a rhinoceros. It even had its horn. "Here we go!" she said brightly, then bit off its head with ruthless satisfaction. *Crunch!*

"Pim!" Mr. Diffy shouted as he walked out the front door.

"Yes, Dad?" Pim sang as she ate the rest of the animal cracker.

Mr. Diffy gestured toward the garbage can. "I keep telling you and telling you to take the garbage out to the curb." He planted his hands on his hips.

Pim sighed. "Yes, Dad," she told him, "but

when you say things over and over like that, they start to lose their meaning."

"That's good to know," Mr. Diffy replied as Pim reached for her soda. Then, his tone turned to a warning. "Pim. Now!"

Pim rolled her eyes and plunked her drink back onto the side table as her father retreated into the house. Slowly, she hauled herself out of her comfy lounge chair and over to the silver garbage can.

Geez! she thought as she struggled to pick the heavy can up. This thing must weigh a hundred metric tons . . . or regular tons, or whatever they say in this time period! She trudged forward about three steps and then gave up, collapsing over the metal lid. "Okay, this isn't going to work," she griped. Pim had no idea how she was going to move the garbage can.

People in this century have huge muscles, she realized. Probably because they have to do all sorts of heavy work . . . like turning on the dishwasher and taking out the recycling. If I were back home in 2121, I could just zap this garbage right out of here, she thought as she looked at the sky.

Hmmm . . . why not zap it? Pim asked herself. Then she smiled. Her genius brain had just come up with a brilliant solution.

She ducked into the family's Fleet Flyer 6000 time machine, currently disguised as a broken-down RV parked in front of the Diffys' home, and carried out a handy little gadget from her century.

"Pim, take out the trash . . ." she muttered, mimicking her father. "Pim, clean your room. . . . Pim, stop talking to yourself. . . ."

The gadget, which looked like a thumb-size rocket, beeped and blinked with a blue light after she twisted the bottom. "I love these penny missiles!" she declared as she attached it to the garbage can and stepped away. A moment later, the missile flashed and went off—and the garbage can shot high into the sky. She laughed as the garbage sailed away, over the neighbors' trees.

Well, Dad, she thought, consider the garbage taken care of. She shook her head. "Trash cans are so last century."

"I saw the strangest reality show last night," Phil told Keely as they walked into Miss Donaldson's class. "*Who Wants to Marry a Dentist*."

Phil shook his head. Reality TV was a purely twenty-first-century phenomenon. He'd never seen anything like it—and he had to admit that it was freakishly addictive.

Keely's eyes widened with excitement. "I did, too. I *so* knew he was going to vote off that girl with that . . ." She gestured toward her teeth with her fingers. ". . . that snaggletooth." She slid into her seat and looked up at the television mounted overhead at the front of the classroom. It was time for a different kind of reality TV.

"Good morning, students," said the bald man on the screen. It was Pim's teacher, Mr. Hackett. He'd just been promoted to vice principal and had taken over the school's public-address system. "Bore-O-Vision," as the students called it, was his brainchild.

"This is Vice Principal Hackett," he went on. "The current temperature is a balmy eighty-six degrees." Mr. Hackett frowned into the camera and gave the students a warning look. "Which is not an excuse for showing off your belly buttons, people," he snapped. "Moving on to sports, last night our gymnastics team won their second straight meet, thanks in large part to the help of Troy Jackaway."

The students in Phil's class erupted into applause as an image of Troy taking a bow behind the pommel horse appeared on-screen. Troy, who was sitting behind Phil, grinned and nodded his head in thanks.

Phil looked at Keely. She was clapping away, smiling at Troy. I never knew Keely cared about gymnastics, Phil thought as a weird feeling fluttered in his chest.

"Troy came away with eight medals in all,"

Mr. Hackett announced, "setting a new county record."

An image of Troy weighted down by medals flashed onto the screen. Coach Buchinsky, the school's physical education teacher and head of the gymnastics program, stared at the medals in awe. "Three," he said, gesturing toward the medals, "four . . . too many to count!" he cried, as flashbulbs went off around Troy. "Too many to count!"

Mr. Hackett reappeared on the classroom's television screen. "Troy," he said, "from one terrific athlete to another: keep up the good work!"

Just then, the vice principal glanced at someone off-camera. "What?" he said defensively. "I *am* an athlete. Ballroom dancing *is* a sport!"

Phil lifted his eyebrows. Okay, some things are pretty different in this century, he thought, but ballroom dancing as an athletic event just doesn't seem right.

On-screen, Mr. Hackett had just glanced back at the camera and realized it was still rolling. "Stop it," he snapped at the camera operator, drawing a line across his throat. "Cut, cut, cut, cut, cut!"

From the front of the classroom, Miss Donaldson shut off the TV and faced the class. "Now that our esteemed Mr. Hackett is through, I'd like everybody to pass up their homework from last night."

From his seat behind Phil, Troy jumped up, placed his homework between his knees, then leaped into a handstand. He delivered his paper to the teacher walking on his hands!

"Wow," Keely whispered to Phil as she gaped at Troy in awe. "Can you believe what he's doing?"

Phil nodded knowingly. "Yeah, he's about to walk where Arnie Hockhausen threw up last week." He shuddered at the thought. I wouldn't want to stick my hand in that, he added mentally.

When Troy reached Miss Donaldson's desk, he stood up and held out his paper to the teacher. Miss Donaldson wrapped him in a huge hug and gave him a peck on the cheek. The class clapped wildly.

What's the big deal, Phil griped to himself. I mean, the homework itself could be all wrong! But the class kept applauding, anyway—everyone except Phil. Who cares if I'm not clapping? he thought as he watched Keely. She's clapping loudly enough for both of us.

Suddenly, Phil got that strange feeling in his chest again. Do I need to go to the nurse's office? he wondered. Or is this what it feels like to be . . . jealous?

CHAPTER TWO

"**W**ashington High School," Troy told a group of kids at lunch later that day. He was sitting on top of a table on the school lunch patio, recounting the details of winning his eight medals. Dozens of kids were hanging around him, staring up at him in awe.

"It's my third and final vault, and I say to myself, I say, 'Bro, you have got one option . . . perfection.'" Troy poked the air to make his point. "So, I go out there and nail it. . . . I turn to the judges and I'm like 'deal with it!'" The multiple medals in his hands clanged together like victory bells as he leaned back and smiled.

"Yes!" cried a redheaded guy named Sterling—one of the many members of the Troy fan club. Sterling held up one of Troy's medals. "Nice anecdote."

Troy nodded at the medal. "Keep it," he said.

Sterling's jaw dropped. He stared at the medal as if it were a giant diamond.

Watching this scene from a nearby patio table, Phil rolled his eyes. "I don't get it," he told Keely. "I mean, first he wins a medal, then he gives it away. What's the point?"

"Hey, I want one," Keely said, ignoring Phil completely. She shoved away her tray, trotted over to where Troy was sitting, and sat down beside him. "Hi," she said, gazing up at him with adoring eyes.

"You want a medal?" Troy asked, handing her one.

"Yeah, sure!" Keely cried. She slipped the medal over her head. She was glad it was attached to an orange ribbon—it looked perfect with her red vest and peach scarf. "Thanks!"

"Hey, looks good on you," Troy said with a smile.

Phil narrowed his eyes as Keely blushed, toying with the medal. Just then, a trash can crashed into the middle of the lunch patio and rolled to the side with a metallic clatter.

Something about garbage falling out of the sky seemed suspicious to Phil, especially for the early twenty-first century. He was *fairly* sure that recycling and landfills were the ways people dealt with garbage in this historical era—*not* spontaneous flight.

The other students didn't appear to notice the arrival of the trash can. They were preoccupied with either their own lunch conversations—or Troy. Keely, for example, was still admiring his medals.

Phil walked over to the flying trash to investigate. Sure enough, there was a penny missile attached to the side of the can, right next to the stenciled-on street address of the Diffys' house. He quickly dislodged the missile and shoved it into his pocket.

Great, he thought with annoyance, all we need is for someone to discover our rocket garbage and find out that we're from the future.

Phil was already learning a lot from watching the movies of this time zone, like *E.T. the Extra-Terrestrial*. He knew that little alien would've been toast if it hadn't escaped on a flying bicycle. And, of course, there were all those movies and TV programs about UFOs and alien abductions.

It seems to me, thought Phil, that every time something weird happens in this era, people call the government. . . . I'd better tell Dad about this right away, he decided, before we're forced to change our address to a remote government compound.

"Wait a minute," Mr. Diffy said as Phil held up the tiny missile, "don't you know what this penny missile means? There could be *other* families from the future here!" He grinned hopefully. "We just have to find them. We just have to make contact with them and we're going home. Boy, we're going home!" he shouted.

Phil winced. He hated to burst his father's bubble, but something about this missile smelled funny—and it wasn't just because it had been stuck to a can of stinky garbage. "Dad, I don't think so," Phil said slowly. "It was attached to one of *our* trash cans."

Mr. Diffy looked confused. "It was?" His left eyebrow lifted as the truth dawned on him slowly. "Pim!"

Ten minutes later, Mr. Diffy, Pim, and Phil climbed into the vehicle disguised as an RV parked in front of their house. "I've called you both into the time machine because Pim may have compromised our security," Mr. Diffy announced.

Pim glared at her brother as they took their seats in the RV.

"So," Mr. Diffy went on, "you've left me no other choice but to lock up all of our future materials. And not in just *any* old box. *This* box." He pressed his hand against a closed drawer, which glowed red at his touch and slid open. Inside the drawer sat a box. "This box is programmed with a lock to read only this beauty." Mr. Diffy tapped his sniffer. "Nose recognition!"

Phil's father stuck his nose "key" into the indentation on the top of the black box to unlock it.

Great, Pim thought in frustration. I'll never manage to break into that thing with my perky little nose!

"Nose verified," the box's mechanical voice announced, "Lloyd Diffy."

The top of the box popped open, and Mr. Diffy dumped in all of the family's futuristic gadgets—the Wardrobe-o-gram, the morpher, penny missiles, and a bunch of other devices.

Pim crossed her arms and narrowed her eyes

at her brother. "Way to go, snitch," she snapped.

"I didn't snitch, all right?" Phil shot back. "I just told Dad what I found."

"Yeah . . ." Pim sneered. *Right*, she thought, like I believe that. More like my perfect big brother couldn't wait to get me into trouble the minute one little trash can crash-landed at school. Big deal! Pim silently howled. It didn't even crush anything!

"Kids, kids," Mr. Diffy warned, holding up his hands. "Hey, that's enough, all right? Pim, as your punishment, you'll be given kitchen duty. That means *dishes*, that means *mopping*."

Pim gritted her teeth. These ancient kitchens were sweatshops! Could there be anything worse?

"Now, if you'll excuse me," Mr. Diffy went on, "I have to go watch *Who Wants to Marry a Dentist*."

Phil and Pim exchanged glances.

"It's idiotic and moronic," Mr. Diffy admitted, "but I can't stop watching it!"

Just like I thought, Phil said to himself. These twenty-first-century reality shows are freakishly addictive!

Phil sighed and turned to his sister. "Sorry about that." He really meant it. After all, now he couldn't use the gadgets, either. He followed his father out the time-machine door.

Pim stayed behind. She didn't care that her brother had apologized. She was at the boiling point. "I *bet* you're sorry, Mr. Never Do Anything Wrong," she muttered through clenched teeth. "One day, you'll mess up and I'll be there. I'll see to it that your reign of goodness comes crashing down like a house of cards!" She grinned at the idea of Phil's ultimate destruction.

"Okay," Phil said.

Pim turned to see her brother leaning against the time machine's door frame. Whoops, she thought. Note to self: stop muttering evil plans out loud.

Phil didn't take his sister seriously. "Uh . . .

make sure you lock up the time machine before you leave," he said, then he turned to go without a backward glance.

That's your *second* mistake, dear brother, thought Pim. Never underestimate your genius sister's ability to execute sweet revenge.

"Hey, Dad," Phil said as he walked into the living room. "Can I speak to you for a sec?"

"Yeah, but you'd better make it quick," Mr. Diffy said in a distracted voice. He was peering out the window. "It's almost time."

"Time . . . for what?" Phil prompted.

"Someone's been watching the house every day," Mr. Diffy said, his eyes locked on the front walk. "I think it's a government thing. And I think they know we're from the future." After all, he'd seen *E.T.*, too. He knew what could happen.

"Okay." Phil took a deep breath, then plunged right in. "See, here's the thing. There's this guy at school who's really good at gymnastics, and everyone seems really impressed with him, even my new friend Keely." He shrugged. "I don't know why it bothers me so much, but it does." Phil looked up at his father, hoping he'd be able to come up with the perfect solution.

"Well, Phil," Mr. Diffy said as he stared through the window, "as a concerned parent, let me ask you . . . how does that make you feel?"

Phil stared at his father for a moment. "I just told you," he said finally. "It *bothers* me."

Mr. Diffy looked at his son. "Then, I think you have two options: one, you can do nothing and be bothered by it, or you can take some action." He gave Phil an absentminded pat on the shoulder as he glanced nervously out the window again. "Son, can we talk about this later?"

"Yeah, yeah." Phil nodded. "I think I know what I'm going to do, Dad."

"Look," Mr. Diffy urgently whispered. He pointed at the front lawn. "There he is. That's him!" Mr. Diffy shoved Phil toward the glass, so he could get a better look.

Phil peered out the window, where a man in a blue uniform was headed toward the Diffys' front door. Of course, Phil and his family didn't know what a letter carrier was. All mail in the future was delivered electronically.

"Uh . . . are you sure he's trying to spy on us?" Phil asked slowly. There was something about the guy—like maybe the funny-looking blue shorts he was wearing—that just didn't say "dangerous spy type" to Phil.

Nevertheless, Mr. Diffy continued to track the man's movements. "Oh, yeah," he told his son. "He'll stop at every house just to make it *seem* normal."

Phil rolled his eyes and patted his father on the back. "You're doing good work, Dad," he lied.

CHAPTER THREE

"**D**ie, you crusty pan!" Pim snarled at the blackened cookie sheet in her hands. Madly, she scrubbed at it, ready to scream. Suddenly, she stopped. Okay, she thought, this is not working.

Pim wore rubber gloves and an apron. Cooking grease covered her from head to toe. She'd been trying to clean this *one* cookie sheet for the last fifteen minutes.

This pan needs to know that I mean business! Pim silently declared. Tossing the shredded sponge aside, she hauled the cookie sheet out of the sink and over to the kitchen island, then started scraping it with a metal spatula.

"How's it going in there with the dishes, honey?" Mrs. Diffy asked as she peeked into the kitchen from the laundry room, where she was folding sheets.

"Oh, just great," Pim said with fake cheer. Once her mother turned her back, Pim carried the pan to an open window and tossed it outside. For the first time since she'd started cleaning the kitchen two hours ago, she smiled with genuine relief. "All done," Pim announced.

"I know it's your punishment, sweetie," Mrs. Diffy said as she walked into the kitchen with a basket full of fresh-smelling laundry, "but isn't it kind of fun doing things for ourselves?"

It had taken Mrs. Diffy a full week to figure out how to operate the washing machine. But that just made it all the more gratifying once she finally discovered how to make it work.

Pim's mom shook her head as she folded Mr. Diffy's pants. "And it's not difficult once you know what you're doing."

Pim gave her mother a sour look as she poured detergent into the dishwasher—the *entire* box of detergent.

Mrs. Diffy didn't notice. "Remember when we used to clean everything with ultrasonic laser light?" she asked with a smile.

Pim's mind conjured up a sweet memory of how she used to take care of the dirty dishes. She'd toss them into the air with glee, and let the ultrasonic laser light blast them into oblivion. "Yeah," Pim said sarcastically, "what was the fun of that?"

Mrs. Diffy handed her daughter a plate of fried chicken. "Could you also put away the leftover chicken, babe?"

"I'm on it," Pim assured her mom. But the second Mrs. Diffy reached for something in the cupboard, Pim yanked open the knife drawer and dumped the chicken inside. She smiled smugly as she shut the drawer with her hip.

"I promised Phil I'd make homemade soup tomorrow night," Mrs. Diffy said as she placed a bunch of bottled spices out on the kitchen island.

Pim planted a rubber-gloved fist on her hip. "Oh, yeah, Phil should have all the soup his little heart desires," she sneered. "'Cause I'm Phil," Pim went on, mocking her brother in a deep voice. "And I'm perfect. And I deserve buckets and buckets of soup!"

Mrs. Diffy gave her daughter a disapproving look. "You know, this isn't about your brother, Pim," she reminded her. Then she grabbed her basket of laundry and headed for the door.

"Well, it *should* be," Pim growled after her mother walked out of the kitchen. "And if it's the last thing I do, it *will* be."

Later that night, as the dishwasher rumbled through its cycle in the kitchen, Mr. and Mrs. Diffy slept peacefully in their bed. But not all of the Diffys were asleep. Phil crept out of his room and down the hall.

In his parents' bedroom, Phil leaned over his father and frowned. I hope I have enough Thompson's Nose Mold Wax, he told himself as he smeared the goo onto his father's nose. With the help of a pair of flashlight goggles, Phil surveyed his work. Not bad, he decided. It's lucky I thought to bring this stuff along in the time machine, he thought. After all, his dad had pulled the old nose-lock trick before.

When the cast was ready, Phil used a pair of metal kitchen tongs to carefully pull it off. Mr. Diffy twitched in his sleep and rubbed his nose.

Phil caught his breath—

But his dad didn't wake up.

Heaving a sigh of relief, Phil grabbed his box of nose wax before sneaking downstairs, through the kitchen, and toward the back door—

"Whoa!" Phil cried, feeling his feet slip out from under him. *Splat!*

He'd just landed in a river of soapy water.

Soapsuds floated down on him like snow. Frantically, Phil checked the wax nose in his hand. He sighed in relief. It was unsquashed.

I think something's up with the dishwasher, Phil thought as he hauled himself to his feet, but I can't stop to check. There's no time. I'm on a mission!

Upstairs, however, somebody else had heard the splat. Pim tossed her bedcovers aside and snuck downstairs. What's my brother doing, sneaking around at this time of night? she wondered as she tiptoed into the kitchen. Whatever it is, it's *his* turn to get busted!

"Whoa!" Pim shouted as her feet flew out from under her and she landed in the soapsuds. Stupid dishwasher! she thought. I hate, hate, hate you! You may think you've won this battle—but just you wait. After I'm through getting even with my smug brother, you're next!

Meanwhile, on the curb out front, Phil opened the door to the family's RV time machine and stepped inside. He pressed the cast of his dad's nose onto his own face.

I just hope this works, Phil thought as he held his hand against the drawer. It glowed red and slid open. Phil leaned over the black box that held the Diffys' futuristic gadgets and pressed his fake nose into the triangular indentation.

"Nose verified—" said the mechanical voice. "Lloyd Diffy."

Phil smiled as the lid to the box hissed open.

From her hiding place by the door, Pim smiled, too. I don't know what you're up to, Mr. Perfect, she thought as she watched her brother take a penny missile out of the box, but I do know one thing. Your reign as Favorite Child is about to come to an end.

The next day, Phil decided to skip lunch. He had something more important to do. He went to the school gym and was about to push open the door when he noticed a handwritten sign posted. NO ADMITTANCE, it read, I'M EATING IN HERE!

For a moment, Phil hesitated. Maybe this sign is a sign, he thought. Maybe I shouldn't do this. . . . But I went to all of the trouble of making the nose cast, he argued with himself. I can't back out now!

Phil looked around. The hall was empty. It was now or never. "It's shoe time," Phil joked with himself as he attached the penny missile to the top of his sneaker, then pulled his pant leg down to hide it.

With a deep breath, Phil pushed open the gym door. "Coach?" he asked as he walked up to a tall, burly blond man.

Coach Buchinsky stood behind a pommel horse, chopping vegetables on a cutting board he'd placed there. Before him was a workout mat laid out with carrots, onions, and scallions. An electric burner sat next to it, warming an enormous pot of bubbling stew.

"Can't you read sign?" Coach Buchinsky

demanded in his heavy accent. "I'm eating home-cooked meal here."

"Yeah, uh . . ." Phil eyed the coach as he turned back to his cutting board. I think it's best if I just pretend like I can't see that, he decided, because I'm pretty sure it's a violation of health and fire codes—in *any* century. "Coach, I don't want to waste your time, but . . ." Phil explained, "I know that you're a busy, uh—"

The coach ignored Phil and continued chopping his carrots.

"—and, uh, *hungry* man," Phil went on, "but I want to be on the gymnastics—" He struggled to come up with the right word. "Thingie."

Coach Buchinsky chuckled and gave Phil a dubious look. "You?"

"People seem really impressed by gymnasts," Phil explained. Especially Keely, he silently added. "So I thought I'd like to be one."

Coach Buchinsky dropped his knife. "What makes you think you can just burst in here and become gymnast?" he demanded, stepping out from behind his gymnastics equipment/kitchen island. "Gymnastics is not like football, huh? Catch ball," he said sarcastically, "run away, touchdown. Rah, rah, rah! Gymnastics is about strength, is about concentration." He poked Phil in the chest. "Is about bravery!"

"Me can do it!" Phil insisted, getting into the coach's whole way of talking about the sport. The coach gave him a raised-eyebrow look. Phil cleared his throat. "I mean, I'd like to give it a try if I could," he finished.

Coach Buchinsky flipped his hand toward the high bar. "You show me," he said, nodding at Phil. "I let pot simmer."

Phil hopped onto the squishy mat and walked over to the high bar. It doesn't look so hard, he thought as he took a deep breath and smiled confidently at the coach.

Rolling his eyes, Coach Buchinsky gave his pot a stir.

Quickly crouching as though he were tying his shoe, Phil activated the penny missile. It flashed blue for a moment, and then Phil yanked his pant leg back over it again.

Satisfied that his soup wasn't about to burn, the coach nodded at Phil to show that he was ready to watch his tryout.

Phil grinned back, and a moment later, he blasted up toward the high bar. He caught hold of the bar as the penny missile did its work, shooting him around and around the bar at lightning speed. Phil imitated some of the moves he'd seen Troy do. Then, once he felt the missile's burst of energy losing steam, he let go of the bar, did a forward flip, and stuck the landing.

"So," he said, smiling up at the coach, "how'd I do?"

Coach Buchinsky's eyes were wide with amazement as he struggled to find the words. "You . . . you . . ." Finally, the coach just shook his head. "You make me want to weep tears of joy!" He held out his arms. "Welcome to gymnastics thingie!"

Phil went in for the hug, but the coach suddenly stopped him. "Look, we celebrate later, all right?" Reaching behind him, Coach Buchinsky pulled a pen and a stapled stack of papers from the rear of his waistband and passed them to Phil. "Right now, we sign release form. Okay. Here. Sign here, and here, over here. You have representation? Down here"—he pointed to the front page—"over here, sign over here . . ."

Phil scribbled his name everywhere the coach asked, unaware that a pair of beady little eyes had been watching the tryout from behind a stack of stretching mats.

"Phil," Pim said to herself as she smiled smugly, "you are *so* busted."

CHAPTER FOUR

" . . . And due to budget cuts," Mr. Hackett announced from Phil's classroom television the next morning, "ketchup is once again a vegetable."

"Who's got the clicker?" Keely called. The kids sitting around her laughed. As if anyone could change the channel, she thought, turning her attention back to filing her fingernails.

"Now, from the world of sports," Mr. Hackett announced.

Phil sat up straighter in his chair. Here it is,

he thought. Finally, my own personal moment of twenty-first-century fame!

"Babe Ruth," Mr. Hackett declared, "Johnny Unitas, Man O' War . . . Phil Diffy?"

Keely stopped filing her nails and looked up. A murmur of surprise rippled through Miss Donaldson's room as Mr. Hackett continued—

"In a story ripped from the headlines, this young athlete has come out of nowhere to help our gymnastics team win tonight as they lock horns with the Westbrook Vikings."

Leaning forward at his desk, Troy grabbed Phil's shoulders and gave him a friendly shake.

Keely turned around in her seat. "Phil, are you kidding me?" she asked.

"Shhh," Phil said with a smile and pointed to the screen, where Coach Buchinsky was talking.

"He is like . . . he is like angel," the coach said in a prerecorded interview, "angel that has flown through window of my tiny apartment."

Standing beside the coach in the school gym, Phil grinned widely. The school's GO ASTRO-NAUTS! banner hung behind him.

"Phil, talk to me," said Vice Principal Hackett. He stepped into the camera frame and thrust a microphone forward. "What's it like being you?"

"I just wanted to join the team," Phil said. "I wasn't expecting all this attention."

Coach Buchinsky spooned up some of his special gym-made soup. "Here. Eat, eat, eat." He shoved the soup into Phil's mouth. "There we go. Good . . ."

"Reporting for the H. G. Wells Witness News Team," Mr. Hackett said, "I'm Neal Hackett, throwing it back to the handsome guy in the booth."

The screen cut back to the vice principal's office, where Mr. Hackett grinned at the camera from behind his desk. "Thanks, Neal," he said, cracking up at his own joke.

Miss Donaldson rolled her eyes.

"On a personal note," Mr. Hackett went on, "this vice principal is so certain that we are going to win tonight, I've gone ahead and made a friendly little wager with Vice Principal Jergens over at Westbrook. Loser has to wear a wedding dress!"

Phil's eyes widened. I know people of this time like to gamble and make wagers, he thought, but wearing a wedding dress? That sounded weird—even to a guy from the twenty-second century.

Mr. Hackett suddenly stared off camera at another person in his office. "What's weird about that?" he demanded.

Miss Donaldson shut off the TV, then turned to face the class. "Good for you, Mr. Diffy!" she declared. As the class applauded, the teacher gave Phil a huge hug. Then Miss Donaldson returned to the front of the room to start class. "Okay, everybody," she said, "let's open our books and turn to page forty-two."

"You never told me you were a gymnast,"

Keely whispered to Phil as they flipped open their textbooks.

Phil shrugged. "It's no big deal."

"Hey, amigo!" Troy clapped Phil on the shoulder once more. "Welcome to the team."

Phil smiled. "Thanks, Troy," he replied.

"All right. Two things." Troy held up two fingers to tick off his advice. "First, nutrition. Two hours before every meet, it's *beaucoup* pasta and salad, got it?" He poked Phil on the back. "Second, it's grooming. You need a righteous hair gel. Now, try this." He handed Phil a clear tube. "See, it's pricey." He fiddled with his own unmoving hair. "But oh, oh, oh, it rocks!"

Phil stared down at the hair gel in his hand. "Thanks," he said uncertainly. But when he looked up at Keely, he saw her grinning at him with admiration.

Wow, thought Phil. Mission Impress Keely is really working!

Later that afternoon, it was Phil who was

surrounded by admirers at the lunch table. "Actually, it's funny," he told his brand-new fans. "I haven't been doing gymnastics long at all. I just kind of took to it."

"Have you given any thought to the 2012 Olympics?" Sterling asked eagerly.

"You know, it's funny," Phil said. "I don't even know where they're being held, but wouldn't it be amazing if we could all be there together? I'm just pitching this, but how about T-shirts?" He spread out his hands, sharing the vision. "Team Phil."

Keely walked up just in time to hear the last part of Phil's speech. She smiled—but it wasn't as big a smile as the one she'd given him earlier that day. *It's strange to see Phil up there, bragging like Troy,* she thought. *Something about it just doesn't seem right.*

"So, what's your secret, Phil?" Sterling asked.

A flash of fear cut through Phil's chest. "Secret?" he demanded. His eyes darted back and forth nervously. *They can't know about the* penny missile, can they? he thought for an instant. "What secret? I don't have a secret."

Brrrrring!

Saved by the bell, Phil thought as he grabbed his black book bag and hopped off the table. "See you later, guys," he called.

Keely eyed Phil's new fan club as they took off for their classes. "Wow, Phil," she said, "impressive entourage."

"Yeah, how 'bout that?" he said, slinging the strap of his book bag across his chest.

"Hey, Phil," called a guy whom Phil had never met.

"Hey," Phil replied, waving hello. Then he turned back to Keely. "I really hope you can come tonight," he told her, handing her a ticket. "I managed to wrangle you a free one."

"Thanks, Phil," she said, and patted him on the shoulder.

Phil tried to look modest about doing this huge favor for her. "No problem," he replied.

"Just so you know," Keely told him, "they're

all free. They stick them in everybody's locker."

Phil tried not to wince. "Yeah," he murmured, even though he actually *hadn't* known that. Man, he griped to himself, and I thought that kid in the hall had totally hooked me up!

CHAPTER FIVE

"**W**elcome to the H. G. Wells gymnastics competition!" the announcer proclaimed over the speaker system.

Phil strode into the gym with his teammates and strutted toward the home-team bench. He was suited up in a sleeveless, blue-and-white H. G. Wells Astronauts uniform. Troy clapped him on the back and gave him an encouraging smile.

I've got this contest locked up, Phil thought confidently as he reached into his gym bag for the penny missile. And now, for my secret weapon. . . .

But when Phil dug around in his bag, he couldn't find the missile. Uh-oh, he thought, where *is* it? Phil shook the bag, then peered inside. But all he could see were sweat socks and a water bottle. The missile was missing!

"Looking for this?" asked a voice behind Phil. He turned to find his sister standing there. Pim had the missile in her hand and a smug smile on her face. "Hello, Philip," she sneered.

Cold fear crept down Phil's spine. "What are you doing?" he asked.

"Just getting the sweet, sweet revenge I promised myself," said Pim, hiding the missile behind her back as Phil grabbed for it. "Oh, and some popcorn," she added, shoving the bag of popcorn toward him instead. "Wave to Mom and Dad."

Turning, Phil saw his parents climbing into their seats in the bleachers. They each held an H. G. Wells Astronauts pennant. They smiled when they saw Phil. Mrs. Diffy waved her pennant.

"What are Mom and Dad doing here?" Phil demanded.

Pim blinked her blue eyes at him innocently. "I guess I *might* have mentioned it to them," she said.

"Why?" he barked.

"I think it's important for Mom and Dad to see their perfect son make a perfect fool of himself," Pim said with a nasty smile.

Phil shook his head. "Do you just wake up evil?" he asked.

She tossed one of her blond pigtails over her shoulder and told him, "As a matter of fact, I do."

"Diffy!" cried Coach Buchinsky, rushing up to Phil. He closely inspected him, then gave him a thumbs-up. "Okay." He trotted off to check on the rest of the gymnasts.

Phil looked at his sister with an expression of sheer misery.

Pim was not moved. "There's just one thing I don't understand," she said to her brother. "*Why* are you doing all this?"

"Hey, Phil," Keely said as she walked up behind him. She was practically bouncing with excitement. "You look good in your uniform. I'm totally impressed." She flashed him a huge smile.

Phil felt a pang. Now Keely is going to know I'm a fake, he thought sadly. Why did I ever think I could get away with this? It didn't help that Keely looked particularly pretty at that moment. Her blond hair was decked out in a cool checkered headband, and the orange shirt she wore under her black jacket made her smooth skin appear to glow.

"Good luck," Keely said to Phil, her hazel eyes shining.

Phil forced a smile. "Thanks," he said.

Pim's eyes narrowed as Keely headed toward the bleachers. "Ohhhhhhh," Phil's sister teased. "You're doing this to impress Little Miss Sunshine."

Phil glared daggers.

But Pim wouldn't stop. "You want her to think that you're a great athlete." She shook her head then pretended to act like Keely, making her eyes wide with fake admiration. "'Wow, Phil. Wow.'"

Phil was ready to choke the little brat, but he was pretty sure strangling your sister was just as illegal in this century as in his own. "So what's your move now," Phil demanded, "rat me out?"

"No," said Pim. Then she handed him the penny missile. Just like that.

Phil frowned at the tiny missile as he turned it over in his fingers. "Why are you giving me this?" he asked suspiciously.

"Because you're devious and evil," Pim said simply. "And you're manipulating people into thinking that you're something you're not." She flashed him a genuine smile. "And I like that!"

Phil wrapped his fingers around the missile. He'd actually felt relieved for a minute . . . but now, the feeling was starting to evaporate. Somehow, having Pim's approval felt worse than being exposed as a lousy gymnast.

"You know," Pim went on, touching her brother on the elbow, "I was never sure we were really related, but now I am." She pressed her forehead affectionately against his shoulder before taking off for the bleachers.

Wow, Phil thought. Pim's admiration is seriously disturbing. He looked down at the missile and sighed.

"Now vaulting for Westbrook," the announcer's voice rang over the public-address system, "Rich Renaldi!"

The audience applauded politely from the bleachers as Rich hit his vault.

That's really impressive, Phil thought as he watched. I mean, Rich just did an incredibly powerful flip off the vault—*without* a missile. I could never do that.

"Next on the vault," the announcer said, "Phil Diffy."

Oh, no, thought Phil. He glanced at the bleachers where Keely sat, smiling at him. She gave him a thumbs-up. A few rows behind her, Phil's parents waved. Mr. Diffy flapped his Astronauts pennant with excitement.

I could make them all proud, Phil thought as he glanced at the missile in his hand. But my victory won't be real. I'm no gymnast. I'm a fraud.

He dropped the missile into his bag and turned to talk to the coach. He had some serious explaining to do.

"This is Phil's first meet as a member of the H. G. Wells Astronauts," the announcer went on. "Good luck, Phil."

"Coach?" Phil tapped Coach Buchinsky on the arm.

"Diffy," the coach said, "you're up."

"No, look." Phil shook his head and swallowed nervously. "I don't think I can do this today."

"Nonsense!" Coach Buchinsky insisted

as he pulled Phil into a hug. The coach gestured toward the vault with his clipboard. "You get in there. Make me weep tears of joy, okay? Okay." He shoved Phil toward the vault. "Go."

Phil hesitated. It looked like there was no way to get out of this. Unless, thought Phil, hope beginning to flare in his chest, unless I actually have some kind of *natural* ability to do gymnastics!

He looked at the judges.

He looked at his parents.

He looked at Keely.

He looked at Pim. . . .

Oh, who am I kidding? Phil thought as he watched his sister cackle with evil laughter. I can hardly make it up a flight of stairs without tripping!

"Uh, Phil Diffy," the announcer said over the speakers, "we're waiting."

Phil took a deep breath. It's now or never, he thought as he headed toward the vault. He ran the short distance to the springing platform, then leaped and—blasted off!

What the heck is this! Phil thought as he felt himself being rocketed higher than he could have ever jumped on his own. That's when he realized what had happened. The penny missile had rolled off the top of his bag and gotten stuck under the vault platform!

Phil found himself heading for the high bar. He screamed like crazy as he spun around and around. He let go and found himself thrown toward the rings. "Whoa!" Phil shouted as he twirled at superspeed. "Whoa!"

In the bleachers, Pim cracked up as Phil went berserk. Coach Buchinsky rushed over to help, but it was no use—Phil was completely out of control!

"Whoa! Whoa . . ." Phil hollered and flailed wildly as he finally let go of the rings. "Oh!" He landed on the coach, sending them both sprawling across a cushioned mat.

Phil raised his arms in the air as the judges

held up their cards. It was a new competition record—0.0 across the board. Worst vault ever.

"Ouchie," Coach Buchinsky complained beneath Phil. "You're on my car keys."

CHAPTER SIX

"**B**ro," Troy said to Phil after the meet, "that was, like, freaky, man."

Troy was once again weighted down with multiple gold medals. "Hey," he continued, "bad jump, excellent hair." Then he clapped Phil on the back and shrugged. "It's something."

As Troy wandered off, the Diffys approached Phil. Mr. Diffy did not look happy. "I just figured out why I woke up this morning with a nose rash," Phil's dad snapped. "You. Me. Home. Later. We'll talk punishment."

Phil grimaced. When his dad started talking like Coach Buchinsky, he knew he was in trouble.

"Hey," Pim said brightly, "if you're looking for a punishment, I've got a bunch of stinky sweat socks." She glared evilly at Phil.

"Okay," Mrs. Diffy told her daughter in a warning tone.

Mr. Diffy draped his arm over Pim's shoulders, and the two of them marched off. But Phil's mom hung back. "Honey," she said gently, "good try. I thought you deserved at least a two." Then she punched him on the arm and smiled.

Phil managed a weak laugh as his mom hurried off.

"Hey, Phil."

He looked up to find Keely waiting to talk to him. Phil swallowed hard. Here it comes, he thought sadly. Now that she knows what a lousy athlete I am, she's never going to want to talk to me again.

"So," Keely said, "what was that thing with the twirling and the, uh, screaming?" A little teasing smile lifted the corners of her mouth. "What was that?" She hitched her bag higher onto her shoulder.

Phil cleared his throat. "Let me be honest with you," he said. "I'm not really a gymnast."

Keely nodded. "Yeah, I kind of figured that out." Her eyebrows drew together in confusion. "But why would you get out there, then?"

"People are impressed by athletes," Phil explained with a shrug. "*You're* impressed with Troy, right?"

Keely sat down on the bench beside Phil. "I'm also impressed by tall buildings," she pointed out.

Phil thought about that for a moment . . . and then laughed.

"So," Keely went on, "you did all this for

me?" She looked around at the gym, where Phil had blasted off like a crazy boy-rocket.

"And for all those kids in the stands who couldn't afford the circus," Phil joked.

Keely giggled. "You know, Phil, I've lived in Pickford my whole life," she said slowly. "Everybody around here is so easy to figure out. But you're not like that. . . ." She looked at him seriously, then her face broke into a smile. "And I *like* that."

Phil returned her smile, relieved.

"So . . ." Keely stood up. "I'll see you tomorrow?"

"Yeah," he said with a nod, then watched her go, thinking, Wow, I guess I don't really need to be a gymnast, after all. Keely likes me just as I am—

"And I *like* that," he said to himself with a smile.

"Congratulations, Vice Principal Jergens, on your school's victory," Mr. Hackett said on the classroom TV screen the next morning. "And on your winning our friendly little wager. We'll get you next year." He shook hands with a tall man in a blue business suit.

Everyone in Phil's class gaped at the television. Their vice principal had actually dressed in a formal white wedding dress, complete with puffy skirt, lace collar, and veil. But he didn't look like a blushing bride. With his craggy face and hairy arms, he looked more like a giant snow creature.

Mr. Hackett peered down at his enormous white skirt. "If I could get some volunteers?" he asked. "I'm going to need some help getting into my car."

Phil just shook his head as he watched.

"You can cut now," Mr. Hackett told the camera operator. "Okay, you know. Just . . . cut. Cut!" A moment later, the screen's picture turned to static.

Keely widened her eyes at Phil, and the two of them cracked up.

Wow, thought Phil, I feel better already. I mean, I may have humiliated myself in front of the entire school by trying to be a gymnast, but at least I didn't have to wear a wedding dress!

LOOK FOR THE NEXT
PHIL OF THE FUTURE!

The Great Fake-out

Adapted by Alice Alfonsi

Based on the television series, "Phil of the Future", created by Douglas Tuber & Tim Maile

Based on a teleplay written by Douglas Tuber & Tim Maile

With a triumphant grin, Phil Diffy tossed the mysterious glowing orb from one hand to the other and then warned his little sister, "Pim, I'm using it first."

"Why?" demanded Pim, stomping onto the back porch right behind her brother.

"Because," Phil replied, "I'm older—" Pim lunged for the orb. Phil jerked it away.

"I'm smarter," he pointed out as she lunged again. "And *taller*," he added, lifting the sphere high over his furious sister's little head.

Being taller was pretty much the reason Phil was holding the orb in the first place. Ten minutes ago, their father had agreed to let them play with *one* device from the future. Mr. Diffy had retrieved the glowing orb from their locked time-travel machine, then threw it into the air. Phil actually caught it before his crafty little sister could get her paws on it—possibly a historical first.

"Phil, you may be taller," Pim replied, "but there's always going to be one thing that I have over you."

"Yeah. What's that?" he asked. "A serious *anger* issue?"

Pim shook her long blond pigtails. "I can hold a grudge *forever*," she declared.

"Oh, really?" asked Phil.

"Yes," said Pim. "Remember the time you ate the last butterscotch pudding cup?"

Phil rolled his eyes. "No."

"Well, you did," snapped Pim. Phil sighed as she recounted the significant details surrounding the incident. "I was four and a half. It was Tuesday. Six thirty-five. You were wearing blue."

Jeez, thought Phil, tossing the orb onto the backyard lawn. Leave it to my disturbed sister to turn a missing pudding cup into the crime of the twenty-second century.

On the grass, the glowing orb began to blink. Then with a blinding flash, it transformed into what looked like a purple snowmobile without the skis. Phil climbed onto the vehicle's seat.

"Pim, I didn't eat your pudding cup," he declared as he gripped the handles of the Skyak and revved its engine. "I put it in your shampoo!"

Before Pim could launch herself at her brother, Phil launched himself into the night air. "Yee-hah!" he cried, then gleefully escaped his sister's fury in a dazzling cloud of Skyak dust.

Pim's foul mood followed her all the way to school the next day.

H. G. Wells Junior/Senior High was a primitive sort of institution where children sat at desks placed in neat little rows and listened to *live* teachers for six or more hours a day.

It was nothing like the virtual classes Pim had attended in 2121. In the future, she'd simply sit in a Comfa-cliner, place her Virtu-teacher visor over her eyes, and let the day's lesson play through her head like a 3-D movie.

Here in this stupid time zone, I not only have to put up with nearly prehistoric technology, thought Pim, I'm forced to interact with annoyingly simple minds—like the one in the hall up ahead.

"Berwick," she growled, walking up to her goody-two-shoes classmate.

Debbie Berwick was wearing one of her typical preppy outfits this morning—a plaid skirt, spotless sweater with matching headband, and string of pearls.

Sheesh, thought Pim, even Sally Sunshine's clothes annoy me! Pim preferred this time period's version of the rebel look. Today she was wearing a PUNK 08 long-sleeved T-shirt, denim skirt, and brown tights.

"Let me guess what's going on here," said Pim, looking Debbie over. "Hot coffee, sports section, standing outside Mr. Hackett's office . . ." The conclusion is simple, thought Pim. "You're either (a) loopy; (b) the world's biggest kiss-up; or (c) a combo platter."

"Pim, I do this for all my teachers," Debbie explained with a big, happy grin. "In fact, would you like to run up a pastry to Ms. Selletti's office?"

Help a teacher? thought Pim. "Uh, no."

Just then, Mr. Hackett's voice leaked out of his office. "I know it's expensive," he was saying, "but I have to have the operation."

Curious, Pim tiptoed to the door and pushed it open enough to fit her ear through. Debbie's smile instantly turned upside down. "Eavesdropping is wrong for seven reasons," she primly announced to Pim. "And I'll explain why. First of all—"

"Debbie, *shush*!" whispered Pim.

"Well, if I don't have the operation," Mr. Hackett went on, "my life will be worthless. Just a big zilch-o."

Debbie's eyes widened in alarm. "Ohmigosh! Pim," she whispered, pulling her classmate back into the hall. "Mr. Hackett is sick and needs an operation. You know what this calls for? A fund-raiser!" Debbie clapped her hands with glee.

"Oh, whoa, whoa, whoa," said Pim, shaking her head. "Every time someone needs help, you're all, 'I'll help you.' And I'm all, 'Get over it.' And you're all, 'To the fund-raising mobile!'"

"Pim, that's okay," said Debbie, her voice full of pity. "Fund-raising isn't for everybody."

Pim frowned as she watched Debbie walk away. "What is she saying? That I can't fund-raise? Well, it's on, Berwick!"

"What's on?" asked Debbie, suddenly re-appearing at Pim's side.

"Stop that!" cried Pim, shuddering. If there's one thing Berwick and her bat hearing can do, thought Pim, it's freak me out!

Meanwhile, inside his office, Mr. Hackett continued to discuss his operation with Maurice, the man on the other end of the phone line.

"The only procedure I can afford is the 106," Mr. Hackett admitted. He picked up the *I Can't Believe It's a Toupee!* brochure on his desk and took a closer look at the "before" and "after" pictures of the procedure he was considering.

"Yeah, that's not a hair-replacement system," Mr. Hackett told Maurice, "that's a toilet-seat cover parted down the middle."

Mr. Hackett listened to Maurice's reply, then declared, "No, no, no. I want it." The teacher took one more look at the brochure—and at the tall, blond women smiling at the man with good hair. "Okay, I *will* still attract big Norwegian women, like the guy on the cover, right?"

Maurice definitely thought so.

"Oh, Maurice," Mr. Hackett cried, "you hound dog!"